The **"Inspired to be..."** book series is a collection of children's books inspired by real people, meant to inspire young readers.

One Flip, Two Flip, Three Flip, Four is the first book of the "Inspired to be..." Series.

This book explores the journey of a child who discovers something that she loves doing. It brings her so much joy that she pushes herself to get better and better at it. As she gets better she starts to dream big and turns this passion into something productive by continuously setting goals and working hard to achieve her dreams.

With this book, it is my hope that children are inspired to be committed to their goals. The sky's the limit when you dream big and work hard to pursue something you love. All you have to do is take it one step at a time.

Crystel Patterson

Inspired to be... One Flip, Two Flip, Three Flip, Four by Crystel Patterson
Imprint: Independently published

ISBN-10: 1087864976
ISBN-13: 9781087864976

*Biographical information on Gabby Douglas cited from
https://www.biography.com/athlete/gabby-douglas

This book is dedicated to Croix and Cylus,
my inspiration for writing this book and the
series as a whole.

- *CP*

It's been a long day, there is nothing to do.

It's raining outside, what's Ruby to do?

She has so much energy,
She can't sit still.
She wants to have fun,
She needs a thrill.

And so it begins...

One flip,
Two flip,
Three flip,
Four...

From the sofa to the floor...

Flipping all around the house,

Landing as light as a mouse.

She flips to the left,

She flips to the right,

She flips all around,

And it's quite a sight...

To her sister who looks on,
And likes what she sees...

Ruby's having so much fun,
She doesn't notice the sun.

A few hours later,
The sun is here to stay.
She really wants to go,
To the park to play.

And so she goes…

One flip,
Two flip,
Three flip,
Four...

She wants to flip more and more.

Listening to the beat of a song,
She can do this all day long.

She flips to the left,

She flips to the right,

She flips with one hand,

And it's quite a sight...

To her mom who looks on,
And likes what she sees…

So Mom makes a decision,
gymnastics Ruby needs.

A few months later,
She attends her first class.
Ruby is so ready,
To learn so much at last.

And so she does...

One flip,
Two flip,
Three flip,
Four...

Studio

She practiced more
than ever before.

Cartwheels, handstands, tucks and pikes,

She trained hard to get them right.

She flips to the left,

She flips to the right,

She lands in a split,
And it's quite a sight...

To her coaches who look on,
And like what they see...

Ruby's really good,
A champion she will be.

A few years later,
She's training with the best.
She's gotten so much better,
The Olympics is her quest.

And so she goes...

One flip,
Two flip,
Three flip,
Four...

Her talent we cannot ignore.
Up against the best in the world,
She has dreams of winning gold.

She flips to the left,

She flips to the right,

She flies like an eagle,

And it's quite a sight...

To the judges who look on,
And like what they see...

Ruby's skills are unique,
She's the winner, they agree.

With her talent and drive,
She knew it in her heart.
Her dreams would come true...

Now, what about you?

This book is inspired by Gabby Douglas, a gymnast who became the first African American to win the individual all-around event at the 2012 Summer Olympics when she was 16 years old. She also won team gold medals at the 2012 and 2016 Summer Olympics. She began her formal gymnastics training at six years old and won a state championship in her home state of Virginia when she was just 8 years old.[*]

Other books in the "Inspired to be..." series:
I am Different
Superheroes Here and There

If you enjoyed this book, please take some time to leave a review on Amazon. Your review makes a huge difference and will help other readers discover this book too.

Thank You!

CPSIA information can be obtained
at www.ICGtesting.com
Printed in the USA
LVHW072219210521
688183LV00002B/16